ALFI AND THE DARK

The illustrations are for Sally, Tony, Alfi
and Frederika, with love

First published in the United States 1988 by Chronicle Books

Text copyright © The Estate of Sally Miles 1988
Illustrations copyright © Errol Le Cain 1988

First published in England in 1988 by Hodder and Stoughton Children's Books
Printed in Hong Kong.

Library of Congress Cataloging-in-Publication Data

Miles, Sally.
Alfi and the dark/by Sally Miles; with pictures by Errol Le Cain.
p. cm.
Summary: On a night when he cannot fall asleep, Alfi meets The
Dark and learns where he goes when someone turns on a light.
ISBN 0-87701-527-9
[1. Dark—Fiction. 2. Bedtime—Fiction. 3. Sleep—Fiction.
4. Stories in rhyme.] I. Le Cain, Errol, ill. II. Title.
PZ8.3.M5774A1 1988
[E]—dc19   88-1043
CIP
AC

10   9   8   7   6   5   4   3   2   1

Chronicle Books
San Francisco, California

ALFI AND THE DARK

by SALLY MILES

With pictures by ERROL LE CAIN

Chronicle Books · San Francisco

Alfi was lying asleep in his bed
When he suddenly woke with a thought, and he said,
"If I switch on the light I'll be able to see
But where will the Dark go? Where will it be?"

The Dark, of course, could hear every word
And laughed to himself and thought, "How absurd
That nobody knows where I go when it's light.
Perhaps, if they knew, it would give them a fright!"

Alfi tossed and he turned and he tried counting sheep,
But try as he might he could not get to sleep.
He sat up and waited, but no answer came.
Then to his surprise someone whispered his name.

"Dark, is that you I can hear but not see?"
A husky voice answered, "Yes, Alfi, it's ME!"
Alfi jumped up and down and he squealed with delight.
"Oh! Where do you go when I switch on the light?"

"I'll tell you," said Dark, "if you don't tell a soul.
But first, tell me, Alfi, where do *you* think I go?"
Alfi tried hard to think but his mind was a blank.
Not one idea came and poor Alfi's heart sank.

"Come on," said Dark, "try not to despair."
Alfi thought for a moment, then jumped in the air.
"If I switch on the light, as I'm blinking my eyes,
You go up and away and are high in the skies!"

There was silence. He waited. "Hey, Dark, did you hear?
Please tell me quick, is it right, my idea?
Dark, won't you answer? Oh, Dark, don't you care?"
But Dark didn't speak for his thoughts were elsewhere.

Dark felt so lonely. Dark felt so sad,
As he thought of the fun and the friends that Light had.
Wherever *he* went people seemed to be scared.
He wanted a friend, just *someone* who cared.

"Why don't you answer me? Why don't you speak?
Are you teasing or trying to play hide and seek?
Answer me, Dark, and you can depend,
I'll keep your secret and I'll be your best friend."

Dark was so happy he laughed with delight.
"Now I'll tell where I go when you switch on the light.
The answer is simple and you'll be amazed —
I NEVER GO ANYWHERE!" Alfi was dazed.

"I'm here in your cupboard, but hard as you try,
When you open the door you can't see me, and why?
'Cause the light gets inside. It's the same with each drawer —
When you let in the light you can see me no more.

"The same with the universe. I'm everywhere,
But when the sun's shining you can't see I'm there.
The moon and the planets, they all know me well.
It's the same with your room. See, I promised I'd tell!"

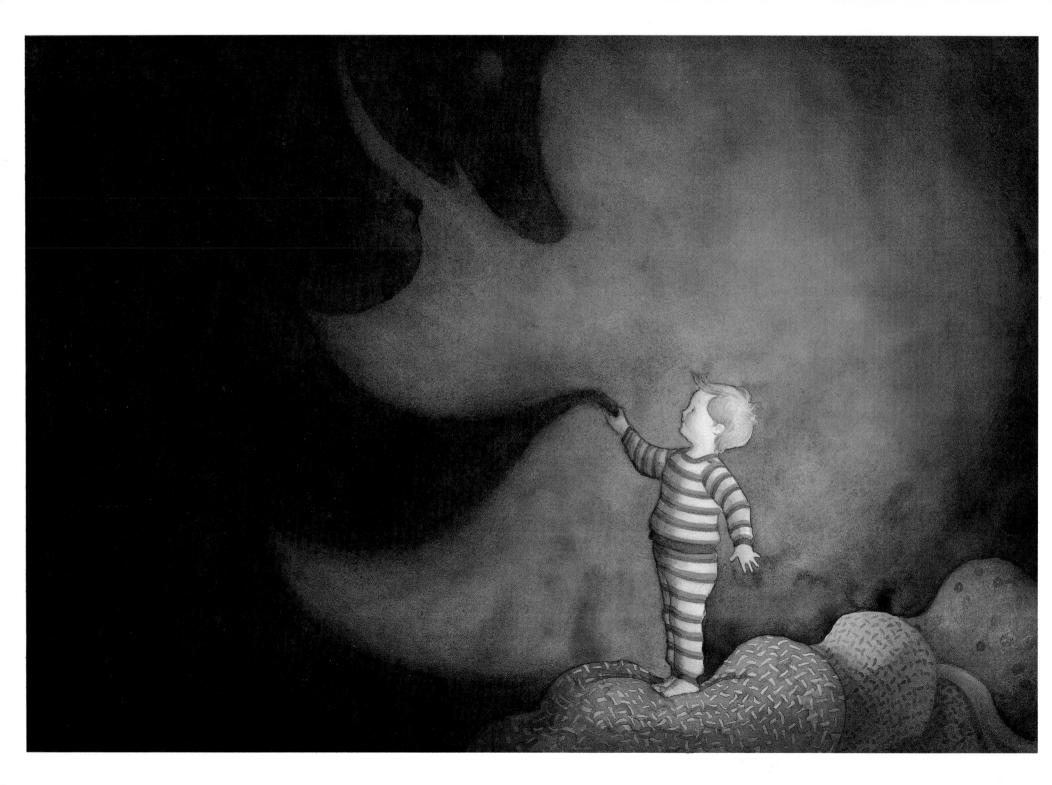

"Oh Dark, thank you Dark, how exciting it's been.
Now I'll never be frightened to wake up and see
That you're there all around me. I'll whisper your name
And know that you'll answer and be just the same."

Alfi crawled back to bed and he snuggled right down.
Then he went fast to sleep without making a sound.
"There," whispered Dark, "lies my very best friend,
Who now knows the answer!" and that is THE END!

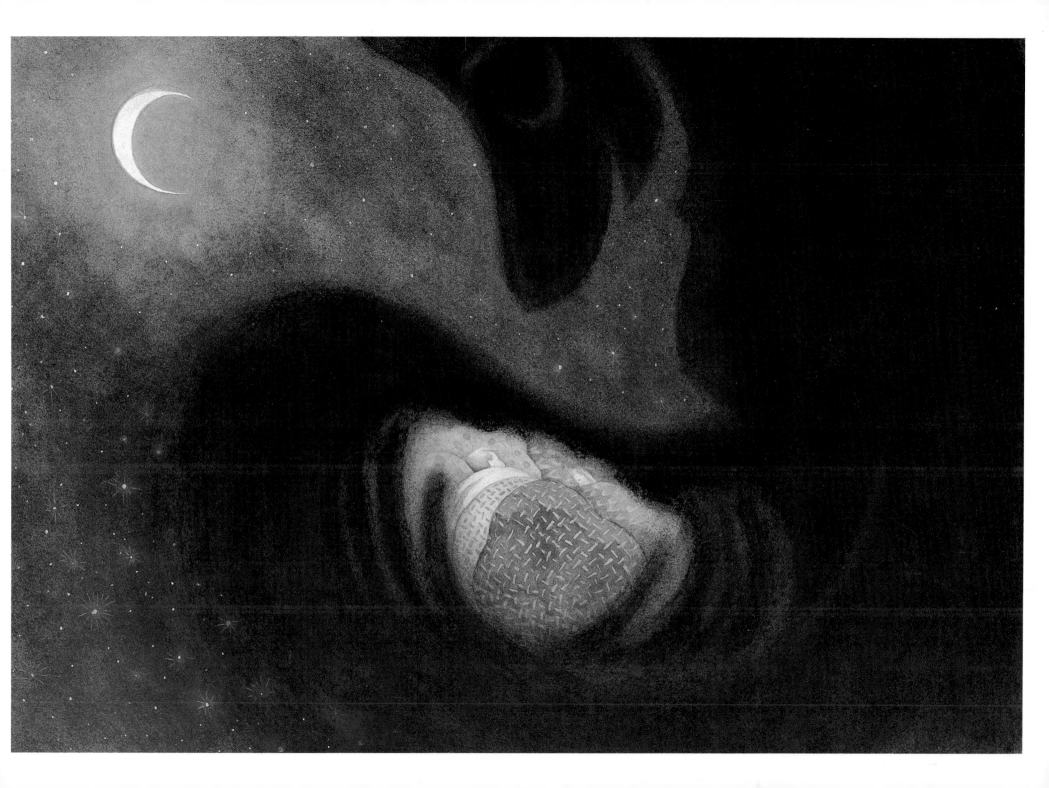

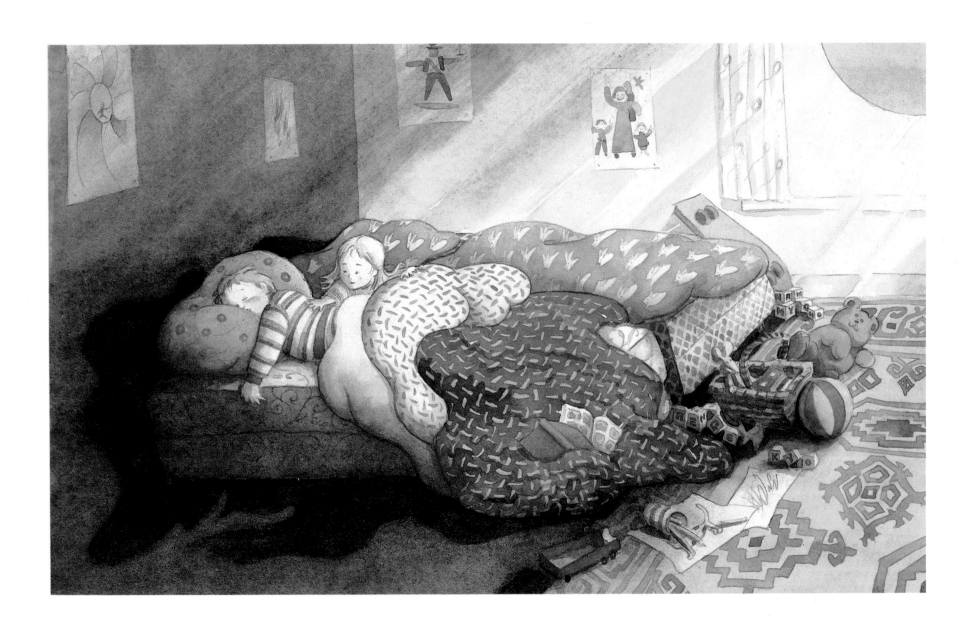